for Adriana!

HAPPY Adventuring!

xoxo IZABEL BZYLAC

The 13th Floor:
Colouring Outside The Lines

story by Crystal Stranaghan
artwork by Izabela Bzymek

This edition first published in Canada in 2012 by Gumboot Books.

Book design by Izabela Bzymek and Crystal Stranaghan, with special thanks to Jared Hunt for his editorial guidance and support every step of the way.

Note for Librarians: A cataloguing record for this book is available from Library and Archives Canada at www.collectionscanada.ca/amicus/index-e.html

ISBN 978-1-926691-25-1

This book printed in the USA.

This is BOOK 2 of the 13th Floor series.

BOOK 1 of the series is
The 13th Floor: Primed For Adventure.
Penelope presses every single button in the elevator of her grandmother's apartment building, and winds up on the 13th Floor. She finds a whole other world when she steps through the first door on the 13th Floor.

Visit us online at
www.crystalstranaghan.com (Crystal)
or **www.faeriesarereal.com** (Izabela)
for more information about this series, and other creative projects by this author and illustrator.

Penelope woke with a crick in her neck,
to Jack's loud meowing as he gave her heck.
She'd slept a lot longer than she maybe should.
They needed to get off of this floor if they could.

1304
eLcOmE
1303
Welcome

Penelope tried the next
door, and another,
but all were still locked,
and she thought,
What a bother!
Then Jack noticed something
Penelope did not.
There was one more door
that Penelope forgot.

Penelope turned the knob
round in her hand,
and the door opened up
to a colourful land.
There were purples and reds
and a very bright blue,
and greens, pinks and
yellows of every hue.

While Penelope stared
through the doorway in wonder,
Jack peeked through her legs,
and then he snuck under.
He went right to the edge,
where the two worlds collided,
and tripped on the doorstep
that kept them divided.

He fell through that door and out into the air,
and Penelope panicked at what she saw there.
He landed far down with a big noisy

splash!

In a rainbow of colour, Jack got a bath.

Penelope froze - what could she do now?
She knew that she had to help Jack out somehow.
With one really deep breath and a quick little prayer,
She jumped through the door . . .
and
fell
through
the
air!

She splashed and she spluttered when she landed all wrong,
but Penelope knew how to swim, and was strong.
She paddled her way to where Jack was last seen,
but when she reached that spot, she let out a scream!

Now the creature had wings,
a beak and strong jaws,
and it rose from the water,
Jack held in its claws.
As they flew up in the air
Penelope cried, "Jack!
I'll save you, I promise,
I will get you back!"

She couldn't run fast enough, and her feet got all bungled,
As the grass by the lake turned into a jungle.
Penelope sat herself down and she wailed,
"If I only had wings, I wouldn't have failed!"

"Well whose fault is that?"
said a voice from a tree,
"Right now you're exactly
what you want to be.

To change in this place,
you just have to decide.
Whatever you want
is reflected outside.

You might wish for wings
or a tail or a snout,
Just give it a try,
you'll soon figure it out.

The trick is to know
deep inside what you want.
You can't get distracted
by doubts or by taunts."

Penelope watched as the creature's shape shifted,
she understood what was possible, and her heart was uplifted.
If she could grow wings and fly high in the air,
she could rescue her friend from that strange creature's lair!

She focused her thoughts on the shape and the feeling,
of wings on her back and flying up to the ceiling.
It didn't quite work, and she flapped and she fluttered,
then crashed back to earth where she angrily muttered,

"You said it would work,
but I did it all wrong.
The creatures that live here
must have minds that are strong."

The creature just laughed
and said, "Change is an art,
and power doesn't come from the mind,
but the heart!"

Penelope thought about
that for a minute,
and this time she really did
put her heart in it.
Her heart wanted freedom,
and wind on her face,
and to rescue her friend
from this strange shifty place.

Penny gave herself monkey arms, perfect for swinging
and the voice of a bird that was lovely for singing.
The nose of a dog meant she could track Jack's scent,
and get her friend back no matter where that thing went.

Penelope flew off
in a flutter of wings,
as she thought to herself,
I can be anything!
She was in such a hurry,
her focus so clear,
When the creature advised her,
she didn't quite hear.

"Be careful!" he called out, "Don't change it all,
Keep a part of yourself that isn't too small.
Your heart's where the power is, and to keep your heart true,
you need to hold on to the things that are you!"

Penny wondered and marveled at each creature she met,
and with each one added something she hadn't tried yet.
Feet that were flippers, the stripes of a tiger,
each Penelope part buried deeper inside her.

She felt powerful, brave, big and so strong!
She transformed herself as she traveled along,
adding all kinds of features to help in the fight.
Some things that would help, and others that might.

Penelope tracked the strange beast to its lair,
and she saw her friend Jack was held prisoner there.
She let out a squawk and made herself big,
and chased after that brute with a sharp looking twig.

She dodged and she stomped
and she squawked really loud.
With all her new skills
she was really quite proud.
She must have looked fearsome -
the creature just ran!
She yelled, "Hurry up Jack,
we must go while we can!"

But when she turned around, Jack wasn't there.
She figured he was hiding, but had no idea where.
Penny searched, and found him terrified and shaking,
his fur all on end and his kitten-self quaking.

Penelope grabbed him and flew them away,
back to the lake where they'd started this day.
When Jack hit the ground, he ran off with a squeek,
and hid behind a bush, risking one little peek.

He cowered and cried
and he whimpered in fear.
With hurt feelings, Penny asked him,
"Why won't you come here?"
Then she caught a glimpse
of herself in the water,
and what she saw there,
well - it truly did shock her!

Of the Penelope she was,
there was no longer a trace,
not a single Penelope
part on her face.
Her limbs and her manners,
her body, her voice-
she'd lost all of herself
with each little choice.

She'd given up everything
to go after Jack,
but now what she needed
was old Penelope back!
She stared at herself
in the watery mirror,
and suddenly everything
all seemed much clearer.

Here in this place you appear as you wish,
as a bird with bright wings, or the fins of a fish.
You are what you wish, on the outside at least.
But the outsides and insides must match to have peace.

Herself was what she really wanted to be,
because nothing felt right, when she wasn't Penelope.
What made her herself? She didn't quite know,
but she knew that it wasn't her shape or her clothes.

She thought really hard, about what she was made of,
and remembered some happy, and one part creative,
many parts mischief, and explorer and chef,
and a few parts of magic and fun were still left.

She closed her eyes tight, and she gathered the parts
that made Penny herself, way deep down in her heart.

When she opened her eyes, her grin grew quite wide,
for Jack was no longer trying to hide.
He jumped in her arms and he licked at her face,
and Penelope said, "Let's get out of this place."

She told him to picture home in his heart,
but when they thought of home, their minds drifted apart.
For Penelope's home, and Jack's, weren't the same,
Jack pictured his family, in a world far away.
They concentrated hard, but when they opened their eyes,
Penelope and Jack were in for one big surprise...

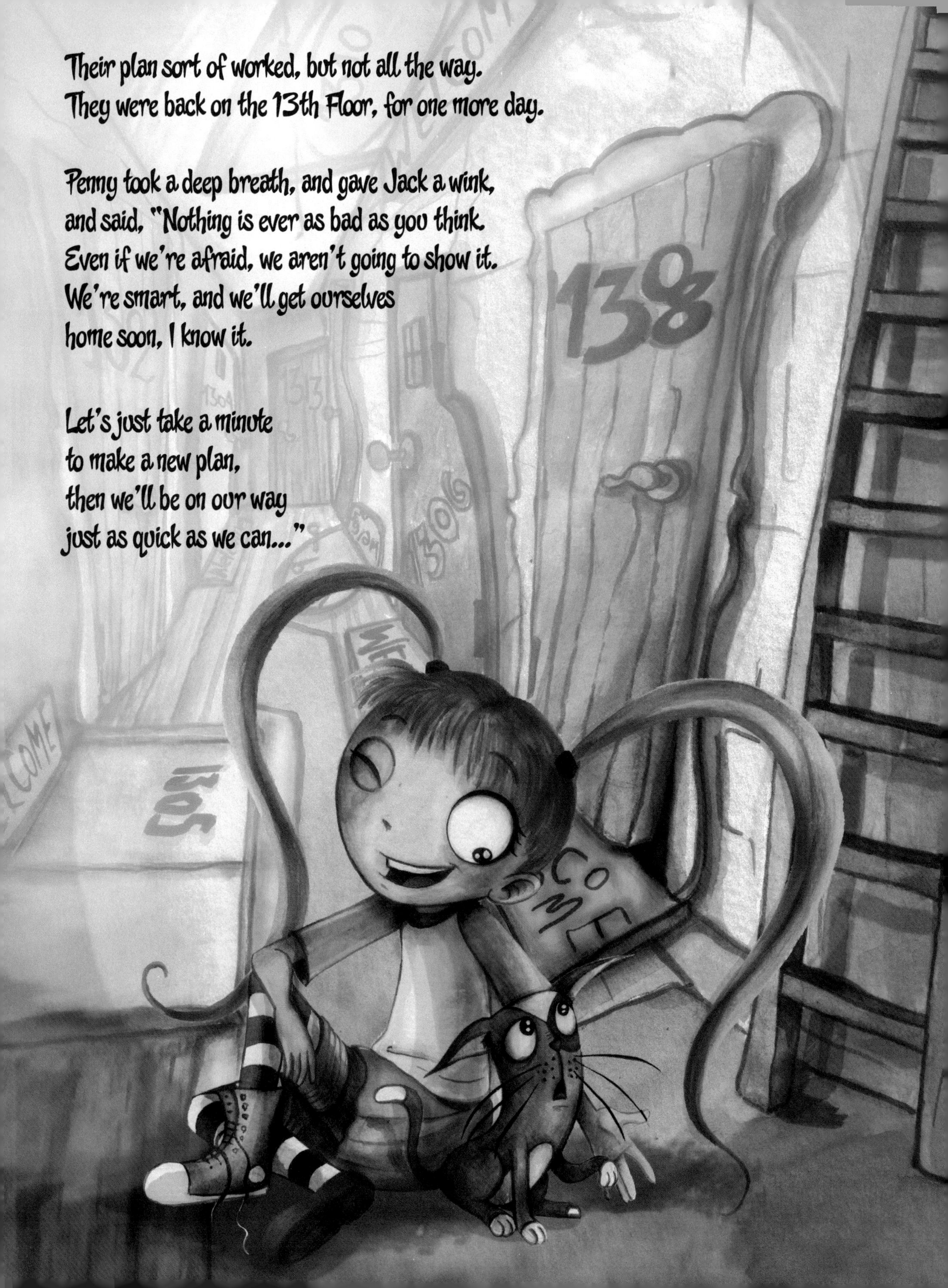

Their plan sort of worked, but not all the way.
They were back on the 13th Floor, for one more day.

Penny took a deep breath, and gave Jack a wink,
and said, "Nothing is ever as bad as you think.
Even if we're afraid, we aren't going to show it.
We're smart, and we'll get ourselves
home soon, I know it.

Let's just take a minute
to make a new plan,
then we'll be on our way
just as quick as we can..."

CPSIA information can be obtained
at www.ICGtesting.com
Printed in the USA
LVIW020755111112
306588LV00001BA